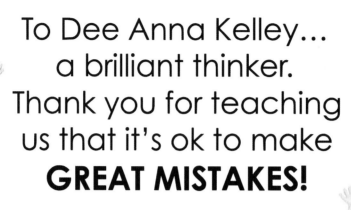

To Dee Anna Kelley...
a brilliant thinker.
Thank you for teaching
us that it's ok to make
GREAT MISTAKES!

Duplication and Copyright

NATIONAL CENTER for YOUTH ISSUES

P.O. Box 22185
Chattanooga, TN 37422-2185
423.899.5714 • 866.318.6294
fax: 423.899.4547 • www.ncyi.org

ISBN: 978-1-937870-43-0   Retail US: $9.95
© 2017 National Center for Youth Issues, Chattanooga, TN
All rights reserved.
Written by: Julia Cook
Illustrations by: Allison Valentine
Design by: Phillip W. Rodgers
Contributing Editors: Jennifer Deshler and Beth Spencer Rabon
Published by National Center for Youth Issues • Softcover
Printed at Starkey Printing, Chattanooga, Tennessee, U.S.A., July 2019

I have **BUBBLE GUM BRAIN.**

I have **BRICK BRAIN.**

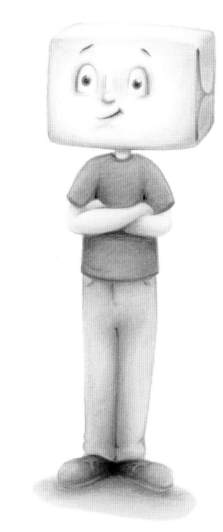

I like to **chew** on my thoughts,

flex, bend and **stretch** my brain,

and **expand** the way I think!

I make

great mistakes

that help me learn.

make great mistakes

With me,

THINGS ARE THE WAY THEY ARE...

and they're probably not going to change much.

I AM THE WAY I AM...

and that's just how it is.

Hey! This looks **FUN!**

This looks **HARD.**

I can't wait to **TRY.**

What if I **FALL?**

6

This takes **A LOT** of balance!

This is **SO** hard!

I love to
play baseball.

Me, too!

I've been working on my hitting.

Relax...
watch the ball all
the way to the bat...
and swing right
through the ball.

Don't strike out!

Don't strike out!

DON'T
STRIKE OUT!

Well, I have the highest
batting average on my team!

I just can't figure this out... **YET.**

THE POWER OF YET

I just can't
figure this out...

AT ALL!

This new song is **SO COOL.**

I hope I can figure out how to play it, because if I can, I'll be able to play just about any song out there.

Then I can **Jammm!**

There's no way my accordion teacher can expect me to play this song!

It's **WAY TOO HARD** for me!

11

Crash! BOOM!

Hey LOOK!
I just made another
great mistake!

SPLAT!

This stinks...**LITERALLY!**

Math homework
isn't my favorite.

Math homework
isn't anyone's favorite.

This math assignment looks
like a brain stretcher...
and it's huge!

It's gonna take some time
to get this one done.

There is absolutely no way
I'm going to get all of this
done by tomorrow. It's way
too hard! Seriously???

**I can't do this!!!
Why even try?!**

I've been working on my free throws in basketball. In the past, I haven't done so well. But now, I practice shooting them every day for 15 minutes so I can get better.

I stink at free throws, but I don't ever worry about that part of my game because I'm super fantastic at defense.

Yeah, but imagine how good you'd be if you were super fantastic at both!

Here I go again.

Only this time, I have an idea!

There is **NO** way I'm ever
going to get this!

This is hopeless! Forget it!!!

Only weird people ride unicycles anyway.

I QUIT!

Studying for my Spanish test all week really paid off! Maybe I should start studying early for next week's test, too.

I totally aced my test! Spanish is easy. I probably won't even need to study for next week's test.

Yes, you do…everyone does.
Your brain only looks like a **BRICK.**
But just peel off your Bubble Gum wrapper,
SEE…it isn't even that thick!

Now your brain
is free to

GROW and
HOPE and
stretch
and **bend.**

Get rid of that fixed mindset of yours,

and the possibilities will never end!

Now that you've peeled off your wrapper,
your **HOPE** can start to **GROW.**

And what you are learning becomes a lot more important,
than what you already know!

You can chew on your thoughts, and stretch your ideas,
and take charge of how you think.

Add a "**YET**" to every "I can't" that you have,
and don't ever stop at "I STINK!"

You need to tell yourself it's **OK** to **make a lot of great mistakes.**

Once you feel
what it's like to have hope,
you'll be amazed at the paths **YOU** can take!

It's not about how much talent you have,
or how much stuff you can do.

What matters most is how hard you work,
at becoming a better **YOU!**

Well, riding a unicycle isn't
going to make me, a better **Me.**

True! But learning how to train your brain
to ride a unicycle will. Besides…it's fun!

Now try it again…only this time,
use your **BUBBLE GUM BRAIN!**

Hey…what if I try this?

WOO HOO!!!

Look how far I went!!!!

OOPS! What I meant to say is, "I wonder how far I can go next time?!"

Now that's more like it!!!

This **BUBBLE GUM BRAIN** thing actually works!

It's really fun to think like this.

*The sky is the limit when my wrapper is off, and my brain isn't stiff like a **BRICK**.*

the Power of YET

I realize now that my mindset's been stuck.
I was caught up in what I was "seeing."

Now I know I must look outside the box,
because **becoming is better than being!**

I get it now...
in order to grow,
there are choices
I need to make.

I need to become
a more hopeful thinker,
and make some **great mistakes.**

I think I'll try to go a little bit farther this time,
and a little bit farther...
and a little bit farther...

Should we try playing our accordions while we ride?

You're kidding, right?!

TIPS FOR GROWING A CHILD'S MINDSET

Ready, Get Mindset... GROW!

Most young children are full of hope and optimism. They think and truly believe they can do anything! But as children get older, they begin to realize that life gets harder. Throughout life, both children and adults tend to cover up their thinking strategies with a "wrapper," inviting a fixed mindset to dominate. As a result, society then tends to deflate optimism, and people end up searching for praise instead of progress.

If we can equip our children with the knowledge and tools needed to maintain their growth mindsets, the possibilities are endless!

Here are a few tips:

- **Great minds make A LOT of great mistakes!**

  Help kids understand that it's not only okay, but also necessary, to make mistakes. Mistakes are learning opportunities that help us grow. When kids can begin to feel safe about making mistakes, they become free to figure out what does and does not work. They also develop more courage to explore new challenges.

- **Avoid blaming**

  When we blame others for our mistakes, we lose an opportunity to learn. Instead, teach kids to own and talk about their mistakes. It's much more important to strive for growth through learning than it is to be perfect.

- **There's more than one-way to "milk a duck!"**

  Every challenge has different pathways leading to the end result. Various problems and tasks require different strategies. Encourage kids to think "outside, inside, around, below and above the box," every time the pathway that they are currently taking is met with an obstacle. Ask open-ended questions that cause kids to look at a situation from different perspectives so that they learn in the process.

- **"Lead the child to water...but don't drink it for them"**

  Often it is easier to tell children how to solve a problem than it is to ask them questions that will lead to genuine problem-solving skill development. Rather than providing kids with the answer, get in the habit of asking, "What's another way that might work to solve this problem?" Asking questions will stretch kids' brains into thinking about problems differently. It will also help them realize they are capable of finding solutions independently, which increases confidence.

- **Teach kids the POWER of YET!**

  Replace "I can't do _____," with "I can't do _____ yet."

- **Encourage and model the practice of not giving up.**

  Oftentimes when solving a problem, the process becomes more valuable than the solution. Developing persistence leads to mental endurance and grows thinking skills.

- **Applaud the effort, but make "IT" ultimately about the learning:**

  Effort is the vehicle to learning and improving. As we help kids realize that a love of learning is far more important than seeking approval, they can begin to develop a growth-mindset that will help them see positives in challenges on the path to gaining knowledge.

  Remember...actions speak louder than words.
  The best way to teach children to develop a growth
  mindset is to authentically model having one yourself!

DEFINITIONS [1]

Fixed mindset: Kids who have a fixed mindset believe their basic abilities, their intelligence, and their talents, are just fixed traits that cannot grow and improve.

Growth Mindset: Kids who have a growth mindset understand that their talents and abilities can be developed through effort, good teaching, and persistence. They believe everyone can get better and smarter if they work at it.

[1] "Stanford University's Carol Dweck on the Growth Mindset and Education." *OneDublin.org*. 2012-06-19.